For my boys,
Jayden and Kirin—
for whom I wrote this story
when they were two.

www.mascotbooks.com

The Crink

<u>For more information, please contact:</u>
Mascot Books
620 Herndon Parkway #320
Herndon, VA 20170
info@mascotbooks.com

Library of Congress Control Number: 2018904985

CPSIA Code: PBANG0718A
ISBN-13: 978-1-68401-204-6

Printed in the United States

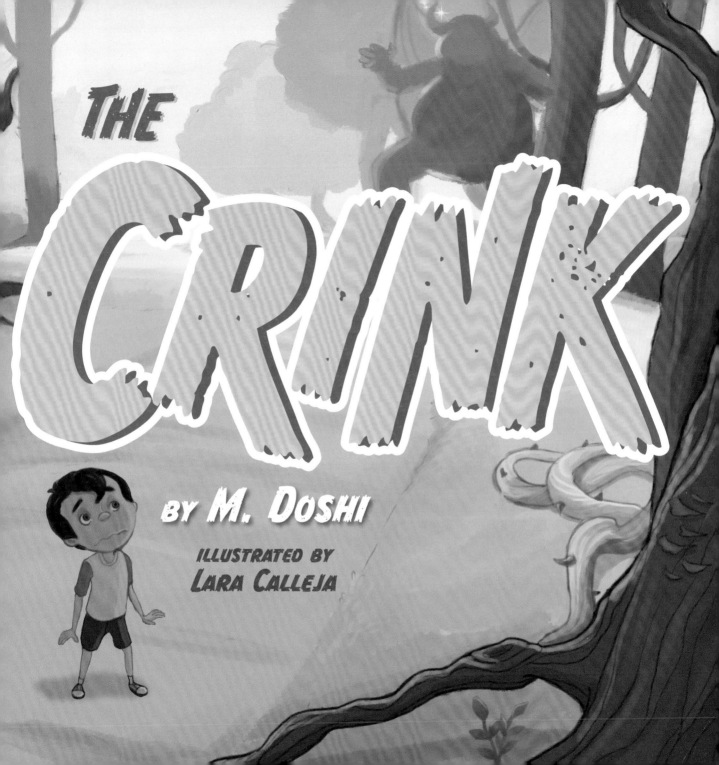

THE CRINK

BY M. DOSHI

ILLUSTRATED BY
LARA CALLEJA

TODObAY I saw a mean old CRINK!
   The worst beast you will find.
Much worse than *geez*...well, anything
   that comes into your mind!

      A creepy troll or ghostly ghoul
         will hide and gasp for air.
      A giant ogre—even he
         would quiver in despair.

A MONSTROUS MONSTER MONSTROSITY,
a Crink will make you sad.
A fiendly **FIEND** of fiendishness,
all Crinks are oh so bad.

So what's a Crink? I think you think,
I'll tell you so you know.
But you'll never leave your house again,
this is a vicious foe!

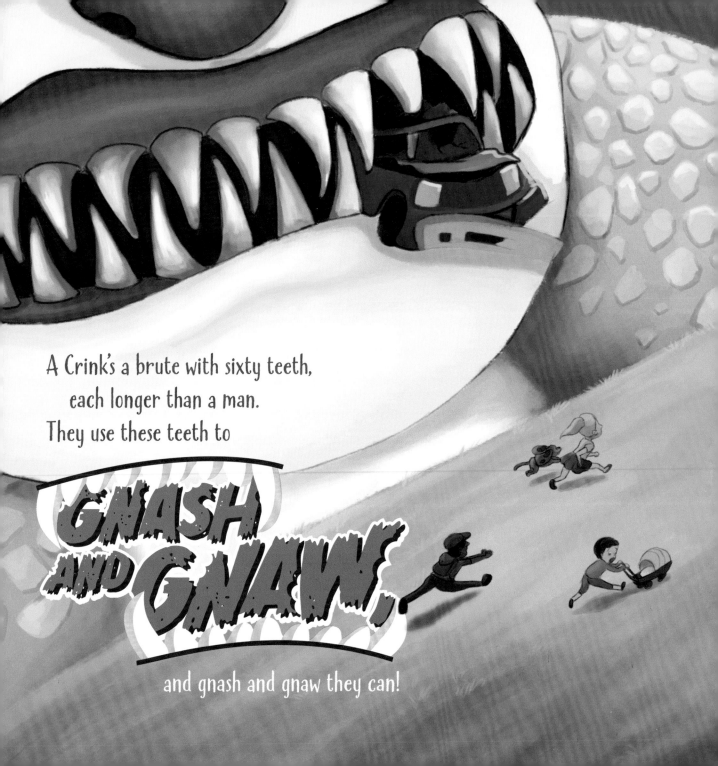

A Crink's a brute with sixty teeth,
each longer than a man.
They use these teeth to

GNASH AND GNAW,

and gnash and gnaw they can!

A Crink has wings that block the sun,
tremendous when they fly!
A Crink has eyes so deeply black,
they'll spot you from the sky.

They've splendid scales instead of skin,
   to shield them from all harm.
They've razor claws from **MAMMOTH** hands,
   a cause for great alarm.

A Crink has horns of EPIC size,
sharp and meant for fighting.
The horns are pink, but even then,
Crinks are not inviting.

A single step with forceful feet,
would split a rock in half.
And did you guess that Crinks are fast?
Of course, don't make me laugh!

WHOOSH!

They have a tail that's full of spikes,
each massive like an axe.
When it crashes down—with a

THUD!

The ground just breaks and cracks.

So should you ever feel a fright,
or sense the grip of fear,
or should you sniff an awful stink,
A CRINK JUST MIGHT BE NEAR.

And if you feel you're on the brink,

or feel your
stomach start to sink,

and if you see
the hint of pink...

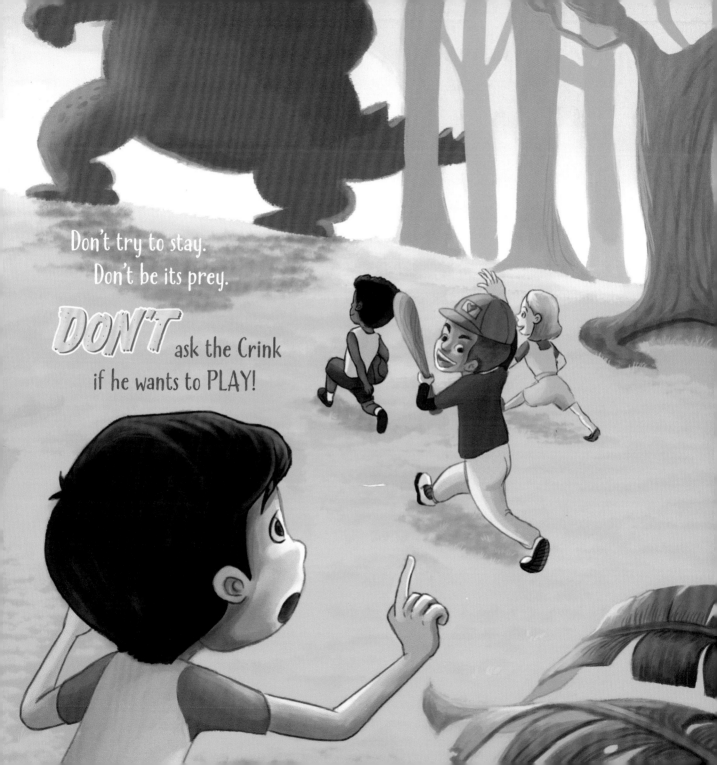

Don't try to stay.
Don't be its prey.
DON'T ask the Crink
if he wants to PLAY!

DON'T try to feel brave today!

Wait, wait, what's that you said?
There are *no* Crinks for me to dread?
The thing I fear DOES NOT exist?
This beastly beast should be dismissed?

I've been in bed the entire day?
I did not leave? I did not play?
I had a cold? I had a cough?
This whole time I've been dozing off?

I felt so scared
I almost froze,

but here I am in
bedtime clothes!